V28/23 KL

A Walk in the Dark
and Other Scary Stories

Read more MISTER SHIVERS books!

MISTER SHIVERS

A Walk in the Dark
and Other Scary Stories

WRITTEN BY
MAX BRALLIER

ILLUSTRATED BY
LETIZIA RUBEGNI

ACORN™
SCHOLASTIC INC.

For my dad. Thank you! —MB

To my love Cristoforo, who always supports me and believes in magic. —LR

Library of Congress Cataloging-in-Publication Data

Names: Brallier, Max, author. | Rubegni, Letizia, illustrator.
Title: A walk in the dark and other scary stories / written by Max Brallier; illustrated by Letizia Rubegni.
Description: First edition. | New York : Scholastic, Inc., 2022. | Series: Mister shivers ; 4 | Audience: Ages 5-7 | Audience: Grades K-1 | Summary: A collection of five scary stories, first featuring Jason, sleeping over at his uncle Henry's house, who needs to take a long, dark walk to the bathroom only to find someone is waiting for him inside.
Identifiers: LCCN 2021045690 (print) | ISBN 9781338821963 (paperback) | ISBN 9781338821970 (library binding) |
Subjects: LCSH: Children's stories, American. | CYAC: Horror stories. | Short stories. | LCGFT: Horror fiction. | Short stories.
Classification: LCC PZ7.B7356 Wal 2022 (print) | DDC [E]—dc23
LC record available at https://lccn.loc.gov/2021045690
LC ebook record available at https://lccn.loc.gov/2021045691

10 9 8 7 6 5 4 3 2 1   22 23 24 25 26

Printed in China   62
First edition, December 2022
Edited by Katie Carella
Book design by Maria Mercado

TABLE OF CONTENTS

Dear Reader,

I like scary stories that make my insides jump—just like the stories in this book.

One damp and cold night, as the old clock struck midnight, I heard something slide onto my doorstep. There I found an old box, covered in melted red candle wax. In the box, I found:

- A cracked pen
- Strands of dark hair
- A hotel towel
- Broken seashells

There was also a notebook with a message taped to its front:

PROMISE ME, MR. SHIVERS, THAT YOU WILL SHARE THE STORIES INSIDE THIS BOOK. OR ELSE YOU WILL BE PART OF THE NEXT STORY.

I'm the sort to keep a promise. So, I now share those stories with you. But here's my warning: they'll make you shiver.

Mister Shivers

A WALK IN THE DARK

Jason was staying at his uncle's house.
The house was big and full of shadows.
It smelled like rotten fruit.

Jason did not want to be there.
The only good thing was that Jason's
uncle let him drink soda.

Jason opened another can of soda
and looked at the long,
dark staircase.

A painting of an old woman hung
above the stairs. The woman had
long white hair and a pale face.
Her eyes seemed to watch him.

5

Jason finished his soda
and opened another.

When Jason went to bed, he rushed
by the painting.

His uncle turned off
the lights.

Jason said, "It's really dark
and the bathroom is
all the way downstairs."

"I'll leave a light on
in the bathroom,"
his uncle promised.

Jason fell asleep.

But he woke up when the old clock struck midnight.

DING. DING. DING.
DING. DING. DING.
DING. DING. DING.
DING. DING. DING.

It rang so loudly the house seemed to shake.

Jason had to pee—**badly**.

"I can do this," Jason said. "I can walk to the bathroom."

He slowly climbed out of bed.

The floor squeaked.

He paused at the door. The hallway was long and full of shadows.

Jason had to pee
so badly it hurt.

He crept down
the dark hall.

He tiptoed down
the creaky
staircase.

Finally, he saw the light.

He was thankful his uncle had left it
on for him.

Jason hurried into the bathroom.

Then he froze.

There, in the bathroom, was the old
woman from the painting. She was
holding a red candle.

Suddenly, cold air rushed past Jason. The old woman's long white hair whipped about.

And the candle blew out as the door slammed shut—**BAM!**

Jason wet his pants.

MY FIRST HAIRCUT

My long, dark hair flowed so far
down my back that I could sit on it.
I loved my hair more than anything.

So, when my mom told me it was
almost time for my first haircut,
I cried.

"But my hair is alive! It's part of me!"
I shouted.

"You can't let it grow forever,"
my mom said. "You're getting
a haircut this weekend!"

I felt sick about the
haircut all week.

When I washed my hair, I heard
a voice in my head:
"Don't let them cut your hair."

When I braided my hair, I heard
the voice again:

"Don't let them cut your hair."

Finally, it was
haircut day.

A bell clanged as my mom pushed
open the shop door. I saw hair
all over the floor.

I heard scissors snapping. **CLIP! SNIP!**
My heart pounded.

I heard the voice again:
"Don't let them cut your hair."

When I climbed into the chair,
I heard the voice again. It was
shouting now.
"Don't let them cut your hair!"

With the first snip, there was
a **scream**!

But it wasn't me who screamed.
It was something else . . .

My **hair** was screaming!

That's when I understood.

There was never a voice in my head
saying, "Don't let them cut your hair."
It was my hair, begging for its life.

Then I started screaming, too.

FINGERNAIL BEACH

Maria was visiting her older cousin
Liz at the beach.

Liz wasn't nice.

Maria stood at the ocean's edge.

A wave knocked her over.
Liz laughed, "Ha-ha!"

Maria played in the sand.
She thought the tiny,
broken seashells looked
like fingernails.

"Look, Liz!" she said.
"Fingernails."

Liz laughed, "Ha-ha! You don't know **anything**! Those aren't fingernails. They're broken seashells."

"I know," Maria said.

Liz laughed, "Ha-ha! Yeah, right."

Then Liz showed off her long nails.
"I bet you think there's some monster
who chews off children's fingernails
and spits them out on the beach!"

Liz laughed again and
Maria nearly cried.

That night, Maria couldn't sleep.
She listened to the ocean waves.

But then she heard a different sound.
A scary sound . . .

Maria crept out of bed. She looked at the moonlit beach and gasped.

Something was moving.
Something big.

A monster was clomping along the shore, spitting something out onto the beach!

Maria dove back into bed and yanked up the covers.

The next morning,
Maria went downstairs for breakfast.

Liz was very quiet. She lifted
a shaking hand to spoon cereal
into her mouth . . . That's when Maria
saw that Liz had no fingernails.

Maria laughed softly, "Ha-ha."

THE FOREVER HOTEL

It was summer. The hot sun beat down as I swam in the hotel pool.

I floated, looking up at the huge hotel. "That's a lot of rooms," I thought.

My dad told me it was time to leave.
But I wanted to keep swimming.

"Can you find your way back to our
room?" my dad asked.

"Dad! Of course," I replied.

As my dad left, he shouted,
"Remember, room 506!"

I swam back and forth across the pool.

I swam underwater
all the way to
the ladder.

I dove to grab a penny
in the deep end.

Finally, the lifeguard said,
"The pool's closing."

When I got out, the air felt like ice.
The sun was setting. I shivered.

"How long was I swimming?"
I wondered.

I wrapped a towel around my body.

My teeth were chattering
as I rushed to room 506.

The door was open, but nobody was
there. I didn't even see our suitcase.

Maybe I had the number wrong.
"Was it 509?" I wondered.

But 509 was empty, too.

39

"I must have mixed up the numbers,"
I thought. "Was it 605?"

I hurried upstairs
and down
the hall.

But room 605 was empty, too.

I was shivering harder now.

I rushed back to the stairwell.

Cold air blew through a vent and whipped around me.

I raced upstairs. My teeth were chattering louder.

I passed room 1001. When I glanced back, the same room said 1100. Were the numbers changing?

I saw a large window at the end
of the hall.

I raced to it, hoping to see someone
outside. The window was foggy.

I wiped it clean. The sky was gray.

No one was outside.

I could see the pool down below.
The water had turned to ice.

I looked at my reflection
in the window.

My whole body was shaking.

I pulled the towel tighter.

As I set off to check room 506 again,
snow was beginning to fall.

THE STOLEN PEN

Nobody saw Robin steal the pen.

When Robin got home, she could not wait to play restaurant.

She used her new pen to take
Mr. Bunny's order:

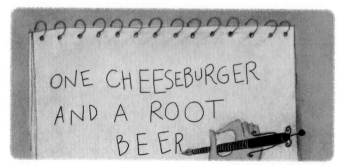

ONE CHEESEBURGER
AND A ROOT
BEER

A second later, Robin's mom appeared.

Robin spun around.
"Mom! Knock first!"

"I have your lunch!"
her mom said. "One
cheeseburger and
a root beer."

"Uh, thanks, Mom,"
Robin said.

Robin stared at the pen.
"Weird! If I write it,
it happens?!"

Then she wrote:

THERE IS <u>NO</u> SCHOOL TOMORROW

A second later,
her brother Lucas
stood beside her.

"Lucas!" Robin cried.
"Don't sneak up on me!"

"A water pipe burst!" Lucas said.
"There is no school tomorrow!"

Robin thought,
"Wow! I wonder if
I can undo it?"

She wrote:

THERE IS SCHOOL TOMORROW

A second later,
her dad
startled her.

Robin's heart pounded.
"You scared me!"

"The pipe was fixed!" he said.
"There is school tomorrow."

Robin thought,
"What should I
write next?"

51

Robin wished
her family
couldn't sneak up on
her anymore!

She wrote:

I HAVE EYES IN THE BACK OF MY HEAD

Robin wasn't worried. She could
always write, "I do **not** have eyes
in the back of my head."

Suddenly, she saw Lucas sneaking in
behind her.

"Get out!" she said.
She saw Lucas pause.

"How did you—"
he began.

"Scram!" Robin yelled.

The eyes in the back of her head
watched him leave.

"With this pen, I can do anything!"
Robin shouted, jumping up.

The pen was knocked from the table.
She pushed her chair to pick it up—

SNAP! Her chair rolled over the pen!

Ink leaked onto the carpet.

Robin scooped up the broken pen and quickly started to write.

But that's all she wrote.

The pen had run out of ink.

ABOUT THE CREATORS

MAX BRALLIER is a #1 *New York Times* bestselling author. His books and series include The Last Kids on Earth, Eerie Elementary, and Mister Shivers. He is a writer and executive producer for Netflix's Emmy Award–winning adaptation of The Last Kids on Earth.

LETIZIA RUBEGNI is a children's book illustrator. At an early age, she fell in love with storytelling through pictures. She carries her red sketch pad everywhere she goes to capture any interesting ideas. She lives in Tuscany, Italy.

YOU CAN DRAW A CANDLE!

1. Draw a wobbly-edged rectangle that has two tall, long sides. This is the candle's wax stick (Use a pencil!) Erase the short, bottom side.

2. Add a thin wick on top. Then draw a circle around the bottom of the candle. This will become a plate.

3. Draw melting wax dripping from the top of the candle. Then add a second circle around the plate.

4. To make the plate look three-dimensional, draw a line below it. Connect that line by drawing two short lines up to meet the edge of the plate.

5. Draw the candle's flame. It is round at the bottom and pointy at its top.

6. Color in your drawing!

WHAT'S YOUR STORY?

A spooky old lady lights Jason's way to the bathroom. The story in this book ends with the candle going out. Imagine what happens next.
What do **you** think the old lady says to Jason?
Write and draw your own scary story!